For my tutor Peter Bailey
with all love and thanks

L. V.

~

May all beings
be happy

Illustrations copyright © 2005 by Louise Voce

First U.S. edition 2005

Library of Congress Cataloging-in-Publication Data is available.

Library of Congress Catalog Card Number 2003069671

ISBN 0-7636-1289-8

10 9 8 7 6 5 4 3 2 1

Printed in China

This book was typeset in AT Amigo.
The illustrations were done in watercolor and ink.

Candlewick Press
2067 Massachusetts Avenue
Cambridge, Massachusetts 02140

visit us at www.candlewick.com

The Quangle Wangle's Hat

Edward Lear

illustrated by Louise Voce

CANDLEWICK PRESS
CAMBRIDGE, MASSACHUSETTS

On the top of the Crumpetty Tree
The Quangle Wangle sat,
But his face you could not see,
On account of his Beaver Hat.

For his Hat was a hundred and two feet wide,

    With ribbons and bibbons on every side

And bells, and buttons, and loops, and lace,

    So that nobody ever could see the face

Of the Quangle Wangle Quee.

The Quangle Wangle said
To himself on the Crumpetty Tree,
"Jam; and jelly; and bread;
Are the best food for me!
But the longer I live on this Crumpetty Tree
The plainer than ever it seems to me
That very few people come this way
And that life on the whole is far from gay!"
Said the Quangle Wangle Quee.

But there came to the Crumpetty Tree,

Mr. and Mrs. Canary;

And they said, "Did you ever see

Any spot so charmingly airy?

May we build a nest on your lovely Hat?

Mr. Quangle Wangle, grant us that!

O please let us come and build a nest

Of whatever material suits you best,

Mr. Quangle Wangle Quee!"

And besides, to the Crumpetty Tree

    Came the Stork, the Duck, and the Owl;

The Snail, and the Bumble-Bee,

    The Frog, and the Fimble Fowl;

(The Fimble Fowl, with a Corkscrew leg;)

And all of them said,

"We humbly beg,

We may build our homes

on your lovely Hat,

Mr. Quangle Wangle,

grant us that!

Mr. Quangle Wangle Quee!"

And the Golden Grouse came there,

And the Pobble who has no toes,

And the small Olympian bear,

And the Dong with a luminous nose.

And the Blue Baboon, who played the flute,

And the Orient Calf from the Land of Tute,

And the Attery Squash,
and the Bisky Bat,

All came and built on the lovely Hat
Of the Quangle Wangle Quee.

And the Quangle Wangle said
To himself on the Crumpetty Tree,
"When all these creatures move
What a wonderful noise there'll be!"

And at night by the light
of the Mulberry moon
They danced to the Flute
of the Blue Baboon,
On the broad green leaves
of the Crumpetty Tree,

And all were as happy
as happy could be,
With the
Quangle
Wangle
Quee.